The Princes' Gifts

The Princes' Gifts

Magic folktales from around the world

JOHN YEOMAN & QUENTIN BLAKE

PAVILION

First published in Great Britain in 1997 by
PAVILION BOOKS LIMITED
London House, Great Eastern Wharf, Parkgate Road, London SW11 4NQ

Text copyright © John Yeoman 1997
Illustrations copyright © Quentin Blake 1997

The moral right of the author and illustrator has been asserted.

Designed by Janet James.

A CIP catalogue record for this book is available from the British Library.

ISBN 1 85793 879 8

Repro by DP Graphics, Trowbridge

Printed in Italy by Giunti Industrie Grafiche

2 4 6 8 10 9 7 5 3 1

This book can be ordered direct from the publisher.
Please contact the Marketing Department. But try your bookshop first.

CONTENTS

THE MAGIC OF FOLKTALES

THE LITTLE-KNOWN FOLKTALES that I have brought together for this book come from very different parts of the world. But, for all that, they have a lot in common.

For one thing, when the stories were first invented they were intended to be told and not read. So they are all much, much older than the earliest versions that I have been able to find in books.

And for another thing, they all illustrate the element of magic which is such a familiar ingredient in most of the folktales that you got to know when you first began to listen to stories. Magic in all its weird and wonderful variations abounds in this book - in the form of wishes granted, supernatural powers, enchanted animals, transformations, the ability to fly, spells, visions, and all those other remarkable things that make folktales so vivid and exciting.

The fact that, whether by coincidence or by direct borrowing, certain of the tales contain moments that remind us of more

familiar stories only increases the pleasure, I think. For instance, we don't mind being able to guess in advance that Aleodor's kindness to the three helpless creatures in *Half-Man-Half-Lame-Horse* will be rewarded handsomely in the end, just as will the young servant's to the old beggar in *The Magic Handkerchief* and the widow's to the old man in *The Pumpkin Tree*.

And I'm sure we all positively relish the age-old satisfaction of seeing the poor, simple characters turning the tables on the mean-spirited people who want to cheat them, as happens in *The Magic Cakes*, *The Witch Boy* and *The Magic Handkerchief*.

It is this marvellous mixture of the familiar and the unfamiliar, together with the colourful backgrounds of the stories, that will - I hope - make these magic folktales worth listening to and reading over and over again.

John Yeoman

Prince Baki
and the
White Doe

Tibet

Once upon a time there lived a young King and Queen who loved each other very dearly. Unfortunately, they were both very argumentative and were always having quarrels. Sometimes the King was right, sometimes the Queen was right. But one thing was certain: neither of them would ever admit to being wrong.

One evening, when they were reclining on their cushions after dinner, the King said, 'Hush! Do you hear anything, my sweet?'

The Queen listened for a moment and then smiled.

'I hear a fox in the palace ground, my love,' she said.

'Not a fox, my precious,' said the King. 'A tiger. You can hear a big tiger roaring.'

'I hear barking, my treasure,' said the Queen. 'Tigers do not bark. That is a fox.'

'This is really too much!' shouted the King, leaping to his feet. 'I will not be contradicted all the time. Summon my counsellors immediately!'

The guards at the door ran off to carry out the King's command and soon the room was full of his wisest ministers and most senior advisers.

At a word from the King they all sat cross-legged on the floor and listened to what he had to say.

'You have been called to decide an important matter of state,' said the King. 'A little while ago, in the palace grounds, a creature began to roar . . .'

'Bark,' said the Queen.

'. . . and Her Majesty and I could not agree whether it was a tiger or a fox. If, in your wisdom, you decide that it was a fox, then I shall submit to being set adrift on a log on the great river that flows by our palace, to be taken where the current wills. If, on the other hand, you decide that it was a tiger - as I am sure it was - my adored partner will undergo the same fate. We leave it to your deliberations.'

The Queen was astonished to hear this and truly thought that her husband had taken leave of his senses.

Left alone to discuss the matter, the counsellors were of much the same opinion. But no one dared say as much.

'It is true,' said one grey-bearded minister, 'that the barking was of a rather foxy kind . . .'

'And the pointed, bushy tail of the beast, which I happened to glimpse,' said another, 'was rather untiger-like . . .'

'Yet all the same . . .' continued a third.

'Yet all the same . . .' the senior minister interrupted, 'if we say it was a fox we shall all be beheaded tomorrow. That confirms my opinion that it was definitely a tiger.'

And so it was agreed. The King was so pleased to hear their verdict that he decided to be generous and give the Queen one last chance.

The next morning, as she placed herself astride the log, he whispered, 'Do you not think you might have been mistaken, my dear?'

'It was a fox,' she said, and pushed herself off from the bank.

After floating with the current for several hours, the log finally came to rest against some rocks on the further bank. The Queen waded ashore through the shallow water and found herself among tall reeds and grasses.

A short distance ahead she thought she could see a wisp of smoke rising, and so she pushed her way towards it. There, squatting beside a small fire, was an old man with white beard down to his waist. He was cooking himself some food.

'Reverend sir,' said the Queen. 'Please be kind enough to spare me a little of your meal. I have been travelling and am very hungry.'

'I know,' he replied, scooping some food on to a leaf and handing it to her.

'I am also lost,' she said, when she had eaten.

'I know that, too,' he replied. 'But you will not be lost for long. You must follow that stony path to the top of the hill, where you will bear a child whom you must name Baki. He will not be like any ordinary child for, from the moment of his birth, he will be able to walk and talk. Great things are expected of him, and you must follow him wherever he leads.'

The Queen was amazed to hear all this but, thanking the old man kindly, she did just as he had instructed.

And, sure enough, she had a child on the top of the hill and the child immediately took charge of things.

'There is no time to lose, mother,' he said. 'Our destiny lies in that direction. Follow me.' And he led her down the hill and through a wood and across a field.

'Let us sit in the shade of this tree,' he said. 'The princes will find us here.'

Now the king of that country had three sons, and it so happened that they were out hunting that day and very shortly passed by the tree where the Queen and her son were resting.

When the three princes heard the Queen's remarkable story, they insisted on taking her and Baki back to the palace with them. The King bade his visitors welcome and not only offered them his hospitality but insisted that he should be allowed to bring Baki up with his own sons. The truth was that he was a widower, and much taken with the beauty of the Queen.

Baki grew rapidly, and in no time learnt the skills of a prince. Soon he was more expert at hunting than his adopted brothers.

One day, when they were all four out hunting together, a beautiful snow-white doe broke loose from the undergrowth before them and bounded towards the mountains.

They straightaway gave chase, but the going was rough and, one by one, the princes dropped back, leaving only Baki in pursuit.

The poor doe herself was becoming exhausted now, and when she came to rest against the face of a cliff, Baki was confident that he had trapped her. But, to his amazement, she lightly touched the rock with her muzzle and it burst open, forming the entrance to a great cave.

As the deer leapt inside, Baki saw that it was suddenly transformed into a beautiful young woman. Without hesitating, he dismounted and slipped into the cave a second before the rock doors crashed together behind him.

Following the retreating form of the woman along winding corridors, he finally found himself in a vast stone hall at one end of which were tall crystal columns.

'What ill-mannered creature are you that intrudes upon the privacy of a lady?' came a voice from behind him.

Prince Baki dropped on one knee before the beautiful young woman and swore that he meant no harm.

'And I hope that no harm befalls you,' she said, in a softer voice, 'for you are now in the hall of the most blood-thirsty ogre.'

'But why are you here?' he asked.

She beckoned him to sit beside her on a stone bench.

'You must know,' she explained, 'that, like you, I am human. The ogre took me captive some time ago and brought me here to wait on him. He hopes that one day I will agree to marry him - but I never shall.

'By watching and listening carefully, I have mastered some of his magic spells but I can never free myself from his while he is alive, and I cannot bring about his death on my own.'

'Tell me what to do,' urged Prince Baki, 'and I will help you.'

'That must wait until tomorrow,' the young woman said, getting up. 'I sense that he is approaching. If he finds you here he will tear you apart and eat you. This is the only place where you can hide.'

She touched the central pillar and it swung open. Baki had only just climbed inside when the sound of crashing rock and footsteps echoing down the stone passageway announced the return of the ogre.

'I'm hungry,' he growled. And then he sniffed the air.

'Human flesh,' he said. 'There's been a human in here.'

'It's your imagination,' said the woman, making him sit down at the stone table. 'See what a fine spread I have prepared for you tonight.'

The vast meal put the ogre in a better mood, and when he had finished, he announced that he wanted some music.

Anxious to please, the lady took up her lute and began to play. Gradually, in time to the music, all the crystal pillars began to glide about in stately dance. All, that is, except the one in which Baki was hiding.

'What's this!' snarled the ogre. 'It refuses to dance for me, does it? Then I'll crush it to splinters with my bare hands.'

The lady was alarmed but her voice was calm. 'My lord,' she said, 'the dance is in your honour. All the lesser columns pay their respect to the great and dignified central column.'

The ogre was satisfied and smiled. In a good mood again now, he curled up in a corner and soon went to sleep.

The following morning he left, early as usual, but announced that he'd be back later to keep an eye on the cave, in case there was a human about.

As soon as he had gone, the lady released Baki.

'It is extremely difficult to kill an ogre,' she explained. 'His body is indestructible unless you can also kill his spirit. And his spirit is always hidden in some other object.'

'And do you know where I can find his spirit?' asked Baki.

'Fortunately he talks in his sleep,' said the lady. 'Behind this cliff there is another tall rock that stands by itself. To enter it you must strike it three times with your right foot and each time you must say *"Great Raven, open the door"*. At the third blow the door will open, revealing a great hall in the centre of which there is a red stone. On this stone is perched a green parrot. Kill the parrot and you will kill the ogre.'

Baki kissed the lady's hand courteously and promised to do all he could to free her. She once again urged him to take care.

Following her directions, he soon found himself before the standing rock. At the third time of his striking the rock with his right foot and calling, *'Great Raven, open the door'* a black shadow passed across the face of the cliff and the two doors flew open, revealing a dimly lit cavern.

In the centre of the floor a stone glowed red, and on that stone sat a great parrot. Prince Baki darted forward, seized it with both hands, and wrung its neck. At the very moment that the parrot squawked its last, there came a choked roar from the entrance of the cavern, followed by the sound of something heavy falling.

Turning, Baki saw the dead body of the ogre sprawled across the threshold, his neck horribly twisted. His hand was still gripping a huge stone axe.

The lady greeted Prince Baki warmly, overjoyed that he had performed his task and had returned safely. Without more ado, the two of them set out on foot to the King's palace.

It was a long walk and the sun was hot and so, at the outskirts of the city, they stopped at an inn to take a bowl of tea.

They could not help overhearing the conversation of two travellers at the other end of the verandah.

'And has the King really passed the sentence of death upon the poor woman?'

'Indeed, he has,' replied the other. 'She has declined to marry him, saying that she already has a husband whom she loves, but the King is too enraged to listen to her pleas.'

'If only Prince Baki were to return soon,' sighed the first. 'Perhaps he could help her.'

'I doubt it,' said the other, with a shake of his head. 'The King, at heart, is a very selfish and cruel man.'

And, fearing they had already said too much, they both fell silent.

Baki's feeling of triumph had turned to dismay.

'How can I save my mother?' he asked the lady.

'Not by doing anything rash,' she replied. 'The spells I picked up from the ogre shall not be wasted. All you have to do is leave me here a while at the inn, set out for the palace at once, and then . . .'

And she whispered in his ear.

Immediately Baki took his leave of her, and hurried off to the palace. Without anyone seeing him, he slipped into the courtyard, sat himself down on the King's mounting block, and muttered some words that the lady had taught him.

At once he was transformed into a large cowrie shell.

One of the guards passing by noticed the shell and strode over to take a closer look.

'That is a remarkably fine shell,' he said to himself.

'Yes, I am rather handsome, aren't I?' said Baki.

The guard leapt back a few paces in alarm. When he had recovered his composure, he approached the shell again.

'And what do *you* know about good looks?' he said sniffily. 'You're only a cowrie shell, after all. You might be a *talking* shell, but you're still only a shell.'

'I know more than you think,' said Baki. 'For instance, I know something about Prince Baki that the King would be very interested to hear.'

Well, of course, when the guard heard this he ran straight to the Palace and told the High Chamberlain who immediately told the King.

On the King's orders, the cowrie shell was brought in and placed on a table before him.

'What's all this nonsense about Prince Baki?' he stormed. 'Come on! What have you got to say for yourself?'

'Only this,' said the cowrie shell. 'If you try to marry Prince Baki's mother or if you try to execute her, you will find yourself in great trouble.'

'Threats!' bellowed the King. 'From an impudent cowrie shell! We shall soon see who is in great trouble.'

And, seizing a ceremonial sword from the wall, he brought the blade crashing down on the shell, smashing it into a thousand fragments.

Imagine the King's horror as he saw Prince Baki rise up before him and each of the fragments turn into a fully-armed warrior.

Seeing themselves so powerfully outnumbered, all the palace guards and the courtiers ran away to hide.

Baki's warriors spirited the terrified King and his sons to a castle at the other end of the country, where they were to remain prisoners for the rest of their lives.

Impressed by Baki's magical powers, all the ministers and courtiers and guards came to bow before him and begged him to be their king. Their work done, the warriors saluted King Baki and, turning into wisps of vapour, drifted up through the ceiling.

To everyone's delight, Baki took the beautiful young lady as his Queen, and they lived happily in the palace for several months.

Then, one day, Baki's mother made a suggestion.

'Your father,' she said, 'has never seen his son nor his daughter-in-law. And, for all his cantankerousness, I would dearly love to return to him. Could we pay him a visit?'

King Baki thought this was an excellent idea and plans were made immediately.

Once Baki's father had become used to the fact that he had a twenty-year-old son who was, in reality, only a few months old, he warmed to his new family. Of course, he was delighted to be with his wife again.

When the time came for Baki and his bride to return home, his mother stayed behind. She lived contentedly with her husband for the rest of their days.

And they didn't quarrel - well, not very often.

THE MAGIC CAKES

China

MANY YEARS AGO, a long way away from here, there stood an inn next to a narrow wooden bridge across a river. No one who lived locally knew anything about the woman who kept the Footbridge Inn, except that she ran it by herself and seemed to be a widow.

The place always looked clean, the terrace was always well swept, and the only noise to be heard was that of the donkeys that grazed in the meadow at the back.

One day, a young merchant happened to be passing along that track on his way to the capital. As evening was beginning to close in he thought he would stay at the inn for the night.

The landlady was most welcoming.

'I have five guests already,' she said, 'and so you will have company at supper this evening.'

And she fetched him a bowl of water to wash with, and then showed him into a room with a blazing fire where the other travellers had gathered to eat.

The meal was tasty and nourishing, and the guests soon felt relaxed and talkative. Some told of their adventures on the road, and others entertained the company with stories which they had picked up on their travels.

At last the young merchant found himself yawning.

'Please excuse me,' he said, 'but I set out very early this morning and must be up at cock crow tomorrow; I really think I should turn in for the night.'

The other guests, all of whom had long journeys to make, agreed that this was a good idea.

'Respected gentlemen,' said the landlady, with a charming bow, 'please allow me to offer you a glass of my delicious wine before you go to bed. I assure you that you will sleep all the better for it.'

The young merchant politely declined, but the other guests thanked the landlady and drank to her good health.

Then she lit a lamp and showed them to the guests' sleeping room on the floor above. There were just six beds in the room, and the young merchant took the one nearest the door.

In a very short while he could hear from their breathing that all his fellow guests were fast asleep. But for some reason - possibly he had eaten too much of the tasty meal - he lay awake.

And then he became aware of something moving stealthily on the floor below. Fearing that thieves might have broken in, he slipped noiselessly from his bed, opened the door a fraction, and peered down into the room beneath.

The landlady was crouching near the dying embers of the fire with a little box in front of her. She took a candle, lit it and then placed it in a candlestick on the beaten clay floor.

What happened next made the young merchant rub his eyes in amazement. She lifted the lid of the box and took from it first a little wooden ox, then a little wooden ploughman, and lastly a little wooden plough.

Then she gently raised a scoop of water from the water bucket,

26

took some in her mouth, puffed out her cheeks, and sprayed the wooden figures with a fine mist.

At once they came to life. In the flickering light the young merchant could see the ploughman harness his ox to the plough and drive it backwards and forwards, furrowing the clay floor immediately in front of the hearth.

When a space the size of a small mat had been ploughed, the landlady drew from her wrap a tiny quantity of seeds which she trickled into the little ploughman's outstretched palm.

He paced up and down the furrows, flinging the seed as he went. Immediately green shoots of buckwheat began to spring up, and the grain began to ripen before the young merchant's astonished gaze.

The little ploughman harvested the grain, threshed it, ground it between two tiny millstones, and handed the flour to the landlady with a deep bow.

At this the little figures turned back into wood again and she replaced them gently in the box.

The young merchant returned to his bed and lay awake all night thinking of what he had seen.

All the guests rose at dawn the next day and gathered their things together, ready for an early departure. There was a mouth-watering smell of fresh baking in the air.

'Respected gentlemen,' said the landlady, 'you would do me a great honour if, before setting out, you would taste one of my buckwheat cakes. I, too, was up early this morning, as you see. They are warm and fresh - and I made them especially for you.'

All the guests bowed politely and accepted - except for the young merchant, who said courteously that he really had to be on his way.

'A thousand pities, gentle sir,' said the landlady sweetly. 'But perhaps you will pass this way again on your journey back from the city. And perhaps I shall be able to tempt you to a buckwheat cake then.'

'It may be so,' said the young merchant, and he settled his reckoning, bade farewell to one and all, and left.

But he didn't start his journey immediately - his curiosity was too strong. Making sure that no one could see him, he slipped over the rail of the footbridge, scuttled along the river bank, and took up a position from which he could watch the back terrace of the Footbridge Inn.

He could hardly believe his eyes. Peering through the leaves, he saw the unfortunate travellers slowly turning into donkeys. First they sprouted long furry ears, then hoofs, then tails, then woolly coats, until they dropped on all fours, looking perplexed. Complete donkeys!

The landlady of the Footbridge Inn calmly ushered the meek creatures into her stables, before returning to collect all their baggage and taking it inside.

The young merchant was so worried that he clambered up on to the bridge again and hurried away as fast as his legs would take him.

His business kept him several weeks in the big city, and during all that time he could not keep the donkeys out of his mind.

As the landlady had supposed, his return journey would take him past the inn again, and on the way he devised a plan.

On the morning before his arrival at the Footbridge Inn, he stopped at a village baker's shop and bought some buckwheat cakes that looked just like the ones the landlady had offered her guests. He didn't eat them. Instead, he put them in his shoulder-bag.

He timed the last part of his journey so that he could arrive at the inn too late for a meal.

The landlady recognized him and was pleased to see him. His baggage was clearly bulging with goods.

'Respected sir,' she said, 'it is indeed an honour to welcome you again. Alas, I can offer you no company at supper this time as I have no other guests in the inn.'

He explained that he had been eating, on and off, all day and would prefer to go straight to bed without any more food. He also declined the glass of wine.

'Then you must have just one buckwheat cake with me,' she insisted. 'I should feel that I have not done my duty as your hostess unless I pressed you to take a little something.'

'It is certainly not my wish to offend,' he replied, bowing deeply, 'but I can really eat no more today. However, nothing would give me greater satisfaction that to try one of your buckwheat cakes before I set out tomorrow.'

The landlady looked extremely contented as she handed him the lamp for him to light his way to bed.

Once again he heard the faint noises from below. He did not look into the room this time but once again lay awake all night.

The next morning the air was filled with the appetising smell of fresh baking and a plateful of buckwheat cakes was waiting for him on the terrace table.

Making certain that the landlady was not about, he scooped the cakes on to a different plate and put the same number of cakes from his own supply on to the first plate.

A little later the landlady appeared.

'But you haven't eaten anything,' she said, disappointed.

'Honoured lady,' he replied, 'since you have been kind enough to offer *your* cakes, I hope you will accept my invitation to try some of mine, poor though they be by comparison.' And he pointed to the plate of her own magic cakes as though they were his own.

She was only too willing to oblige him, and raised one to her lips with a smile, while he helped himself to one of the baker's cakes.

For a moment her eyes stared into his as she waited for the transformation to begin, but then her eye-lashes grew longer and flickered, and her ears grew longer and twitched, and she turned into a gentle, but sturdy, donkey.

'I had better take the box of little wooden figures,' said the young merchant to himself, 'although, since I have no idea how the magic works, I cannot lift the spell from the travellers.'

But he did release all the donkeys into the meadows so that they would not starve.

Then he took a harness from the stables and fitted it on to the landlady-donkey. To his surprise, she proved to be very docile and very strong. He bundled his goods into side packs and set off back home at a much faster pace and in greater comfort than before.

For a few years the young merchant rode his donkey whenever he took a business trip. But one day, in a remote part of the country, he saw an old Sage asleep on a stone bench by the wayside. As he drew up to him, the old man suddenly lifted his head and said, 'Bless my soul, if it isn't the landlady of the Footbridge Inn!'

The young merchant was far too astonished to ask him how he could tell.

The old Sage rose and patted the donkey's muzzle. 'Young man,' he said, 'your donkey has been good and obedient. These years of faithful service have surely made up for the wrong that was done. Let us set her free.'

And with that he removed the bridle, and at once the donkey's form began to dissolve. The landlady of the Footbridge Inn stood before them.

To the old Sage she gave a deep bow, but to the young merchant she merely gave an empty look. Then she turned and walked away.

Nothing has been seen of her in that part of the world since.

THE WITCH BOY

New Mexico, USA

MANY YEARS AGO a boy lived with his grandmother outside a village. They were very poor, but they were quite contented: the grandmother took good care of the boy, and he took good care of her.

He also grew very fond of a girl who lived in the village. When she was grinding corn he would come to her window and talk to her, and she enjoyed his company.

But there was another boy who was also interested in the girl. He lived in the village too, and looked just like any ordinary boy, but he wasn't. He was a witch boy, and nobody knew.

He, too, used to visit the girl but, try as he might, he couldn't get her to say sweet things to him. She was always polite when he called, but it was clear that her heart was set on the other boy.

This made the witch boy very angry, and he decided to get rid of his rival. Pretending to be very friendly, he stopped to talk to him one day as the boy was collecting sticks for his grandmother's fire, and asked him if he'd like to go hunting.

'I know where there are plenty of rabbits,' said the witch boy, 'and I have a very special way of catching them, which I'll teach

34

you, if you like.'

'That's very good of you,' said the boy, not suspecting anything. 'There's nothing my grandmother likes better than rabbit for supper.'

'I promise you she'll have her rabbit,' said the witch boy. 'In fact, we'll probably catch so many that you'll have some to sell in the village. But, first of all, you've got to promise not to tell anyone what you're doing. It's a secret.'

Of course, the boy promised willingly, and they agreed to meet at a certain remote spot later that afternoon, at the time when the rabbits would be feeding.

They met at the appointed place, and the boy was eager to start.

'What's your special plan?' he asked. 'Do we use a net?'

'Better than that,' replied the witch boy, with a sly smile. 'We change ourselves into coyotes by jumping over this,' and he produced a small hoop from behind his back.

The boy looked rather doubtful, but the witch boy was very persuasive.

'No rabbit stands a chance against a coyote,' he reasoned. 'In no time we'll have as many rabbits as we can carry, and then we'll quickly change back and be home in good time for supper.'

To show what he meant, he placed the hoop on the ground, jumped over it and immediately changed into a coyote. The boy did the same and was amazed to find that he, too, had changed into a coyote - with a tempting smell of rabbit in his nostrils.

Almost immediately he spotted a rabbit feeding a little distance away and gave chase. It took him no time at all to get used to hunting the way coyotes do, and it wasn't very long before he had heaped up a tidy pile of dead rabbits by a rock.

Satisfied that the boy was too busy with his hunting to notice anything else, the witch boy jumped over the hoop, changed back into human shape again, scooped up some of the dead rabbits in his arms and, picking up the hoop, set off home.

He laughed out loud to himself as he trotted along.

'Not a bad afternoon's work,' he chuckled. 'Not only have I got free rabbits for supper, but I've also succeeded in getting rid of my rival. The poor fool will have to stay a coyote for the rest of his days while I visit his girl as often as I please.'

When the boy thought he had collected enough rabbits for the two of them he looked around for his friend and realized that he was nowhere to be seen.

At first he was puzzled. Then he began to get a bit anxious. And later, when it had grown dark and he couldn't find his friend - or the hoop - anywhere, he became seriously alarmed.

'What am I to do?' he wailed. 'I can't stay like this!'

Eventually he decided to slink into the village under cover of darkness in the hope of finding his companion. But as soon as he came within sniffing distance, all the dogs set up a dreadful howling and a few of them chased him off, back into the scrub.

Meanwhile, his old grandmother waited and waited and worried and worried. She knew he was not the sort of boy to stay out without telling her what he was doing.

At first light the next morning she went into the village to ask if anyone knew anything.

'Have you seen my grandson?' she asked a group of boys. 'He didn't come home last night.'

The witch boy was among them. He pretended to think for a while, and then said, 'Ah, yes; I remember. I passed him yesterday afternoon. He said he was off hunting.'

And she had to be content with that.

For days and days after that the boy roamed the scrub looking desperately for his supposed friend.

He was in a wretched state. He could not eat raw meat like real coyotes and he was afraid to try to light a fire in case the villagers saw the smoke and came to investigate, or set the dogs on him. In fact, he grew so weak and miserable that he would have died if the eagle spirits hadn't taken pity on him. From their place in the sky they had seen everything, and decided that the time had come to help.

They sent their swiftest eagle down to fetch him.

'Have no fear, young man,' said the eagle. 'We know that you became a coyote through trusting a false friend. Although your grandmother is now sick with grief and your false friend is singing his praises to your girl, all will be well. Climb on to my back. The eagle spirits are waiting for you.'

The boy needed no persuading. He scrambled on to the eagle's back and found himself borne higher and higher, with the wind whistling through his fur.

Once landed, the eagle spirit led him into the Great House where the Chief Eagle was sitting in state. The hall was crowded

with eagle spirits - men, women, boys and girls - all without their eagle feather coats, for they take them off and hang them on the wall when they are at home.

'Welcome to the village of the eagle spirits,' said the Chief Eagle. 'We shall return you safely to earth, never fear.'

At a signal from the Chief Eagle, one of the eagle spirits fetched some hot water, while another dragged a large earthenware jar into the middle of the floor. The boy was lifted into the jar and the hot water was poured in. Then the Chief Eagle took a dried herb, the roots of which were in the form of a great hook, and twisted it into the coyote skin on the boy's head. Muttering some secret words, he gave a violent heave and pulled off the coyote skin in one movement.

The boy was his former self again.

The eagle spirit boys washed him all over and dressed him up in a splendid new outfit of soft buckskin and eagle feathers. Then the eagle spirit girls washed and combed his long hair until it shone in the firelight. After that they all sat down to a great feast that lasted, on and off, for four days.

At the end of that time, the Chief Eagle clapped his hands for silence.

'You have now grown strong and well again, young man,' he said, 'and so the time has come for you to return to your own people. You shall take with you not only our blessing but this deer which we have killed for you, and this herb medicine.'

The eagle spirit men slung a deer across the boy's shoulders and fastened a small buckskin bag of herb medicine to his belt.

'Your false friend is no other than a witch boy,' the Chief Eagle continued. 'When you arrive he will be anxious to meet you, to find out how you changed back from a coyote. Say nothing, and behave naturally. Invite him to a meal of freshly killed deer. And then, when he sits down to eat, sprinkle the herb medicine on his meat, and justice will be done.'

They all helped the boy on to the eagle spirit's back again, and in no time he found himself among the rocks outside the village.

At his grandmother's house, he flung down the deer and cried, 'Grandmother, I am back!'

When the old woman raised her head from her blankets and saw him standing by her side she almost fainted for joy. Although she had been very ill indeed for the past few days, the very sight of him soon had her on her feet again.

The news of his return spread quickly and, just as the Chief Eagle had predicted, the witch boy was the first caller.

'It is good to see you back, my friend,' he said; 'I was getting worried. You must tell me exactly what happened.'

'I decided to hunt deer,' the boy replied. 'In fact, I caught a fine one and would be most honoured if you would join me in a feast tomorrow.'

The witch boy couldn't understand, but since his rival seemed so friendly and trusting, and since there was the prospect of a hearty meal, he accepted the invitation readily.

The following day the witch boy turned up in good time. The delicious smell of cooking that was hanging in the air put him in a very relaxed mood. He chatted away cheerfully to his host, thinking that he was an even bigger fool than he had first suspected. But he didn't notice the boy sprinkling a little of the herb medicine on his meat while he was pouring himself some water.

There was no immediate change. It happened gradually. First the witch boy found himself pushing his face into his plate to feed himself, then he realized he was lapping up water from the jug with his long tongue, and then he started scratching behind his ear with his foot.

'Oh, no. I've turned into a coyote!' he would have cried, if he'd still been capable of human speech. As it was, all he could do was throw back his head and howl.

With no idea of what was happening, the grandmother rushed in and chased him into the street with her broom. Once the local dogs caught his scent they all came running, sending him fleeing into the distant scrub to save his life.

The boy knew that all the dogs in the neighbourhood were first-rate guard dogs; they would never let a coyote anywhere near the village. And that meant that the witch boy would never be able to reach his hoop and change back into a boy again.

The boy went on visiting the girl until there came a time when they decided to get married. And then they both came to live with the grandmother and were all very happy.

In fact, the only thing that ever disturbed them was that sometimes, at full moon, they were kept awake by a lone coyote howling in the distance.

MOTHER WHIRLIGIG'S DAUGHTER

Norway

THERE WAS ONCE a widow with a son so lazy and pleasure-seeking that he could think only of singing and dancing from morning to night. It was bad enough when he was young, but the older he grew the more he ate and the less he did for himself.

'You're eating us out of house and home,' his mother said in despair one day. 'Why don't you go out and look for work?'

'Look for work?' he repeated. 'Oh, I don't like the idea of that at all. Oh, no; I'd rather woo Mother Whirligig's daughter than work. For if I could win her, I'd eat well and live well, and sing and dance to my heart's content for the rest of my days.'

His mother thought that this really wasn't such a bad idea, seeing how bone-idle he was. So she made him put on his Sunday best, brushed him down, polished his shoes for him, and sent him off to Mother Whirligig's house. The lad set off, singing and dancing, saying that he was going to take the short cut.

Although the sun was shining brightly, it had rained the night before, so the turf was like sponge and there were pools everywhere.

'I'll leap from hillock to hillock,' he thought, 'so as not to dirty my nice clean shoes.'

Singing at the top of his voice, he sprang from one tuft of grass to another, and splash! he disappeared from view completely. When his eyes became accustomed to the darkness, he was annoyed to find himself in a damp tunnel at the bottom of a deep, dark hole.

Then he heard a jingling sound, and a rat came wiggle-waggling towards him with a bunch of keys tied to the tip of her tail.

'Here at last, my sweetheart!' she cooed. 'I, too, have waited anxiously for this moment. But let us be patient for just a little longer and I shall bring you the finest dowry you could ever hope for.'

The youth was just about to say, 'Never mind that nonsense, how do I get out of this stuffy hole?' when she continued: 'But do forgive me, you must be starving. Pray eat your fill before you go.'

To the youth's disgust, the rat put before him a pile of broken eggshells and vegetable peelings and scraps that people scrape off their plates after a meal. He knew that she meant well and he

didn't want to offend her, especially as he needed her to help to get back above ground, so he tasted a little for the sake of good manners.

'And now you'll want to be on your way,' said the rat. 'Believe me, I know how your heart is set on the wedding, and I promise to make all haste.'

'*Only get me out of here and you'll never see me again,*' thought the lad. But he merely smiled politely.

'You must take this linen thread,' she said, 'and sing the tune I teach you. And when you are above ground you must be sure to go straight home, and never look behind you until you are there.'

She then sang:

'*Spin the thread and weave away,*
Soon will come the wedding day.'

It was a catchy tune, the kind of tune the boy was fond of dancing to. As soon as she had finished, he echoed her with a hop and a skip and found himself above ground.

He didn't need any reminding to dance his way straight home. He wanted to get away from the rat hole as quickly as possible.

'*Spin the thread and weave away,*
Soon will come the wedding day'

he sang, bounding from tuft to tuft.

His mother was there to greet him at the gate, with her hands clapped to her cheeks in amazement. There, behind him, stretched out as far as the eye could see and a little bit farther, was a length of the whitest, finest linen.

Together they hauled in the linen, singing and dancing and unable to believe their luck. The widow cut it up skilfully to make shirts for her son and blouses for herself, and what they couldn't use she sold in the market at a very good price.

For a while they lived extremely well, but there came a day when both the larder and the purse were empty. Once again, she suggested that he might look for work.

'You know, mother,' he said, 'I'd still rather marry Mother Whirligig's daughter.'

The widow thought that it was an even better idea now, for the lad looked very smart in his bright new shirts. So she brushed his Sunday best, polished his shoes for him, and sent him off to Mother Whirligig's house.

The youth set off singing and dancing but, remembering what had happened last time, he decided to take a different short cut.

Once again it had rained the night before and so he had to jump very carefully so as not to dirty his nice clean shoes.

Suddenly, splosh! he disappeared from view completely. To his great annoyance he found himself at the bottom of another hole, and there was the rat wiggle-waggling towards him with the bunch of keys tied to the tip of her tail.

'Back so soon, my sweetheart?' she cooed. 'Of course, I am flattered to find you so eager, but some things simply cannot be hurried. I promise you, though, that everything will be arranged by the time you next visit me, and I know that you'll think the dowry was worth waiting for.'

With great difficulty the youth prevented himself from saying, *'There won't be a next time if I can help it.'*

'But, poor love,' she went on, 'you must be starving.' And again she begged him to take his fill of her disgusting feast of left-overs.

He made a pretence of enjoying the little that he put to his lips, and this seemed to please her well.

'And now you'll want to be on your way,' she said. 'Please don't fret over the delay. You can trust me to hasten things on as fast as ever I can.'

'Then get me out of this damp-smelling hole right now,' he thought. But he merely smiled politely.

'You must take this woollen thread,' she said, 'and sing the tune I taught you. Be sure to go straight home, and never look behind you until you are there.' Together they sang:

'Spin the thread and weave away,
Soon will come the wedding day'

and he found himself singing and leaping along, on his way back to the cottage.

His mother, waiting at the gate, was even more amazed. There, behind him, stretching out as far as the eye could see and a little bit farther, was a length of the smoothest woollen cloth.

Together they hauled it in, singing and dancing and unable to believe their luck. The widow lost no time in making the smartest jackets and breeches for her son and some warm winter cloaks for herself, and what they couldn't use she sold in the market at a very good price.

For a while they lived extremely well, but once again there came a day when both the larder and the purse were empty. The widow told her son that it really was time that he went out and looked for work.

'I still think my best bet would be to marry Mother Whirligig's daughter,' he replied.

The widow agreed that that would be far the best plan, now that he had got his fine new suits to go courting in. So she brushed his smartest woollen jacket and breeches, polished his shoes for him, and sent him off to Mother Whirligig's house.

As usual, he set off singing and dancing, and determined to take a short cut over good, solid ground. But it had rained very heavily the night before and so he had to make some extra big leaps to avoid dirtying his nice clean shoes.

Suddenly, splosh! he disappeared from view completely. He was more annoyed than ever to find himself at the bottom of yet another hole. And there was the rat, wiggle-waggling towards him with the bunch of keys tied to the tip of her tail.

'Welcome, sweetheart!' she cooed. 'I guessed you would come today to claim me. I fully understand your impatience, and I am happy to tell you that everything is ready for the wedding. You will be delighted to hear that we can set out for the church at once.'

'Just get me above ground and we'll see who can run the faster,' he thought, but he didn't say anything.

Then the rat whistled, and from out of the darkness there came swarming rats and mice of all shapes and sizes. Some of them harnessed six of the stronger rats to a frying-pan, and two of the mice climbed on the back as footmen, while another two climbed up in front to drive. Then some of the lady rats helped the bride to her place on the frying-pan carriage.

'The ways are rather narrow down here,' the rat said to the youth, 'and so I must ask you to crawl on your hands and knees before the carriage - just until we reach the open air. Then you can sit beside me,' she added with a simpering smile.

The lad had his own ideas about what he might do when he reached the open air, but he thought it best not to mention them.

The passage was indeed narrow, but he closed his eyes and squeezed himself forward as best he could.

Suddenly the youth found himself above ground and heard a sweet voice behind him say, 'Our way is clear now. Perhaps you would like to join me in the carriage.'

Turning round he had the surprise of his life. There stood the grandest golden coach, complete with six white horses and liveried attendants, and in it sat the most beautiful maiden he had ever clapped eyes on.

'I am a princess,' she told him, 'put under a cruel spell with all my waiting women. But because you came to visit us and never said an unkind word against us, that spell is now broken. Shall we drive on to the church?'

Now the lad quickly reckoned that this promised a whole lifetime of singing and dancing, and told her that this was all right by him.

So they drove off in style to get married and then drove off in style to the princess's magnificent palace. And another grand coach was sent to collect the delighted widow.

Never had that part of the country seen such wedding celebrations. In fact, they are probably at them still, and if you're quick you may be just in time to join in the singing and dancing.

THE MAGIC HANDKERCHIEF

Georgia
(former USSR)

A LONG, LONG TIME ago there was a rich old miser and his wife who lived in the depths of the country. Although they were incredibly wealthy, they were also very mean and never gave anything to help the poor people round about.

For years they ran the house all by themselves, because they couldn't bear the thought of anyone seeing their possessions, and being tempted to steal them.

But one day the old woman sighed and said, 'I sometimes think it would be nice to have someone to help me clean the silver and beat the carpets and prepare the meals. I'm not getting any younger.'

Her husband looked up from the pile of coins which he was counting.

'My mind has been running along the same lines,' he confessed. 'But think of the expense, and think of the worry of having a stranger in the house.'

They both fell silent for a while. Then, at last, the wife spoke. 'Perhaps we could find some young orphan,' she suggested. 'She wouldn't need much to eat, and she could sleep in the stable.'

'That's it!' said the husband. 'She'd hardly cost us anything, and you could thrash her from time to time to remind her to be grateful to us for giving her a home.'

And so, the very next day, the old miser rode off to the town and returned that evening with a young orphan girl.

She was very frail and very frightened, but she was truly grateful that these people had taken her under their roof.

'Here's your supper,' said the wife, handing her a bowl of stale rice and a mug of water. 'And eat it slowly. We don't want you getting fat and lazy.'

In the following months the girl worked from morning to night, with never a word of complaint. She polished the floors, washed the clothes, fetched the water, cooked the meals, and never had a moment's rest. At night, she slept outside in the stable.

Even the mean old wife had to admit to her husband that she was a treasure.

'The place has never been so clean and tidy,' she said, 'and she doesn't cost anything to feed. What she eats is only what I'd have to throw away if she weren't here.'

'That's true,' said the old man, smiling. 'But don't tell her how good she is, or she'll get conceited.'

'Don't worry; I shan't,' cackled his wife. 'I still knock her head against the wall and pull her hair from time to time, to keep her in her place.'

As the months passed, the poor maidservant began to grow weak and ill from too much work and too little food, but still her master and mistress shouted at her for her laziness.

She took it all meekly and never complained. But deep down inside she was very unhappy.

One day, the wife said to her husband, 'I've been noticing how beautifully our maid mends all the tears in her threadbare clothes. She's obviously a first-rate seamstress. If you took me to town I could buy some lengths of silk for her to make into gowns for me. Think of the money we'd save.'

The husband agreed that this was an excellent idea, and so they set off immediately, leaving the girl a whole heap of jobs to do before their return.

As soon as they had gone, she looked at herself in the mirror and sighed at the change that had taken place.

Her hair was lank, her skin looked unnaturally pale and her hands were red and chapped. For a moment she felt like crying, but she pulled herself together and started to clean the pots and pans.

She worked and worked the whole day, without even stopping for a bite to eat, for she knew how angry the master and mistress would be if she hadn't completed her chores by the time they returned.

Her last job was to heat the stove. For fuel she had to use rice straw, and it usually happened that a few grains of rice would fall out of the straw when she took it from the basket.

Food was so precious to her that she used to pick up these grains and put them into a little bag. As she closed the bag she realized that she had enough now to treat herself to a bowl of freshly-cooked rice for a change.

A knock at the door made her jump. She immediately felt guilty, because she had been told time and time again that she wasn't to let anyone inside the house when her master and mistress were absent.

But when she half-opened the door and saw the stooping figure of an old beggar standing there, she immediately felt sorry for him.

'My kind young lady,' he said in a cracked voice, 'I haven't eaten all day, and am faint with hunger. Please ask your mistress if she could spare a bowl of food for an old man.'

'Reverend sir,' said the maidservant, 'my mistress is not at home and I'm afraid that she would refuse you even if she were. But if this little bag of rice would help you, you are welcome to it, I'm sure. It's not much, I know.' And she blushed with shame as she pressed the bag into his upturned palms.

In a voice that seemed slightly less quavery, the old beggar replied, 'It is much more than I had reason to expect, my dear. I, too, have little to give. Only this handkerchief. You can use it when you wash your face. But be very careful not to let anyone else have it.'

He bowed and walked away, with a spring in his step which surprised the girl.

She had no sooner tucked the crisp little handkerchief into her sleeve and turned to go back indoors when she heard her master's voice behind her.

'So that's what you get up to when we're away, is it?' he bawled. 'Encouraging beggars and riff-raff!'

'You'll pay for it,' said his wife, panting up beside him. 'You'll go to bed supperless, this evening. That'll teach you a lesson!'

The maidservant bowed meekly. It was no more than she was used to.

That night, alone in the stable, she dipped the handkerchief in her basin of cold water and wiped it over her face. It felt surprisingly refreshing.

Every night for a week, before she went to bed, the girl washed her face with the old beggar's handkerchief.

'I can t believe it!' gasped the mistress to her husband one morning. 'Our maid has been transformed. Just look at her.'

His wife was absolutely right. The girl's skin had a healthy glow, her eyes sparkled, her hair was silky, her hands were soft and elegant, and she moved with grace and beauty.

'What have you been doing to your face?' the old woman demanded to know.

At first the girl couldn't think what she was talking about.

'Nothing,' she said. 'That is, every night I just wash it with a cloth which the beggar gave me.'

'Bring me that cloth,' the old woman squawked.

While the maidservant was fetching it the old woman turned eagerly to her husband.

'Don't you see,' she cried, 'it must be a magic cloth that gives the user eternal youth and beauty. If we used it, we could become young again and lead a life of luxury for ever and ever!'

'Give me that cloth,' the old man demanded, when the maidservant returned.

'I was told that I mustn't . . . ' she began, apologetically.

'Don't argue with me!' said her mistress, snatching the handkerchief out of her hands.

Straightaway the mean old couple squatted down by a bowl of water and began to wash their faces and hands with the cloth.

At first, they were chuckling with delight, but after a while the old man said, 'Doesn't it feel a little rough on your cheeks, my dear?'

The old lady agreed that it did.

'And the backs of my hands are feeling a bit itchy,' she said.

'Mine seem to be getting uncomfortably hairy,' said her husband, sounding very anxious indeed.

They loped over to the mirror to see what was happening and discovered, to their horror, that they had both turned into monkeys.

Gibbering and screeching with rage and humiliation, they bounded out of the house and off into the mountains. They were never seen again.

And the girl, a maidservant no longer, lived happily in the house on her own.

THE PRINCES' GIFTS

Portugal

T HERE WERE ONCE three princes who were all great friends. Each of them was preparing to go on a long journey and, on the day before they set out, each chanced to see and to fall in love with a beautiful maiden looking out of her window.

The first prince, without telling the others, sent her a note saying that he must see her before he set out. She sent a note back to say that he might visit her at six o'clock, if he chose.

The second prince, without telling the others, sent her a note saying that he must see her before he set out. She sent a note back to say that he might visit her at six o'clock, if he chose.

The third prince, without telling the others, also sent her a note saying that he must see her before he set out. And she sent a note back to say that he too might visit her at six o'clock, if he chose.

When the hour arrived, the princes were upset to discover that the maiden had invited them all at the same time.

'It is clear that you care for none of us,' said the first prince, 'since you invited all three of us together.'

'Not at all,' replied the maiden. 'I like all three of you very much.'

'But you can only marry one of us,' said the third. 'Can you not tell us which one you will choose?'

'You are all so fine and charming,' said the maiden, 'that I cannot find it in my heart to like any one of you better than another. But since you must have an answer, I shall be happy to marry whichever one of you brings back from his travels the gift that pleases me most.'

They had to be satisfied with that, so they thanked her kindly and took their leave.

A few days later, when they reached the crossroads where they had to part company, they wished each other well and agreed to meet at the same spot on their way home.

The first prince arrived at his destination and straight away set about finding a precious gift to take back for the maiden. One day, he saw a great crowd of people outside a glass-maker's shop and joined them to see what was going on. The glass-maker was holding up a looking glass and saying:

'This is a truly amazing looking glass. There is not another like it in the whole world. You have only to say to it, "Looking glass, I wish to see such-and-such a person" and that person immediately appears, reflected in it.'

The prince knew at once that this was the only gift for the maiden, and bought it for a bag of gold coins.

The second prince arrived at his destination and straight away set about finding a precious gift to take back for the maiden. One day he saw a great crowd of people outside a rug-maker's shop and joined them to see what was going on. The rug-maker was holding up a strangely-patterned rug and saying: 'This is a truly amazing rug. There is not another like it in the whole world. You have only to say to it, "Rug, take me to such-and-such a place" and it will instantly transport you there.'

The prince knew at once that this was the only gift for the maiden, and bought it for a bag of gold coins.

The third prince arrived at his destination and straight away set about finding a precious gift to take back for the maiden. One day, he saw a great crowd of people outside a candle-maker's shop and joined them to see what was going on. The candle-maker was holding up a simple white candle and saying: 'This is a truly amazing candle. There is not another like it in the whole world. You have only to place it between a dead person's hands and say to it, "Candle, bring so-and-so back to life" and that person will instantly be alive and well again.'

The prince knew at once that this was the only gift for the maiden, and bought it for a bag of gold coins.

The day arrived when the three princes had agreed to meet at the crossroads. Each was eager to show his companions the wonderful gift which he had bought to win over the heart of the maiden.

The first prince held up his looking glass. 'Prepare to be amazed,' he said, and he commanded the glass to show him the beautiful maiden.

Imagine their distress when there appeared in the glass the reflection of the maiden, lying dead on her bed.

'All may not be lost,' said the second prince, unfolding his rug. 'Perhaps there is still a glimmer of life in her. I can transport us to her instantly and we can summon the best doctors to revive her.'

He commanded the rug to take them to the maiden. No sooner had they stepped on to it than it rushed them through the air, and in no time they found themselves standing at her bedside. But it was clear that she was quite dead.

The third prince took his candle and placed it between her

fingers. He then commanded it to make her alive and well. The maiden blinked her eyes, sat up, and smiled to see the three princes again.

'We are delighted to see you restored to life,' said the third prince. 'And since it was my gift that revived you, I beg you to remember your word and marry me.'

'But it was my gift,' said the second prince, 'that transported us here in time, so I beg you to remember your word and marry me.'

'But it was my gift that told us that you were dead,' said the first prince, 'so I beg you to remember your word and marry me.'

'You all three have my undying gratitude,' said the maiden, 'and you all three have a claim to my hand. But since I cannot marry three husbands, I shall not marry any of you.'

The beautiful maiden went away to shut herself up in a tower. And the three princes, sadly disappointed, did exactly the same.

HALF-MAN-
HALF-LAME-HORSE

Romania

A LONG, LONG TIME ago, when bears had long tails and hawthorn bushes were covered with sweet pears, there lived an old Emperor.

His wife had died, and his pride and joy was his son, Aleodor. The courtiers all agreed that it was only the old man's delight in watching Aleodor play, and hearing him chattering with the counsellors and the gentlewomen of the palace, that kept the old Emperor alive for so long.

But finally the old man knew that his hour had come. He called Aleodor, now a young man, before him and made his last farewell.

'My son,' he said, 'there is nothing I can tell you about ruling these lands after me. From your tenderest years you have shown yourself to be wise and caring. But there is one warning which I must give you and which you must heed. Never set foot upon the mountain which you see in the distance. All the rest of these lands are yours, but that grim mountain belongs to the fearsome Half-man-half-lame-horse, and no one who offends him lives to tell the tale.'

Shortly after this the Emperor died, and while his people

mourned the passing of the old man, they counted themselves fortunate in having the new young Emperor to rule over them.

Aleodor, by his thoughtfulness and fairness, fully earned the high esteem in which his counsellors held him. But not all his time was spent on affairs of state. In his spare moments there was nothing he enjoyed better than to ride his horse across the countryside and feel the wind blowing through his hair.

One day, however, he was galloping along with his mind on other things, when his horse suddenly neighed in alarm and reared up on its hind legs.

Too late, Aleodor saw that his way was blocked by the hideous creature known as the Half-man-half-lame-horse, and he realized that he had strayed absentmindedly into the forbidden territory.

Aleodor was immediately filled with regret, not so much at what the foul beast might do to him, but at having ignored the advice of his dying father.

'Villain!' snarled the Half-man-half-lame-horse. 'What right have you to trespass on my property?'

'Please forgive me,' said Aleodor calmly. 'It was certainly wrong of me to enter your territory, but I beg you to believe that it was not done deliberately.'

'A likely story,' growled the monster, dribbling down its chin, 'but, whatever your excuses, you are on my land and I mean to exact my punishment. You shall die like all the others.' And his claw-like hands began to twitch and his misshapen hind leg began to paw the ground.

Aleodor slipped nimbly from his horse. 'I am not looking for a fight,' he said, 'but I am prepared to defend myself if I have to. Shall it be with swords, or clubs, or shall we struggle hand-to-hand?'

An evil glint came into the twisted creature's eye. 'You are a foolish young man, but you do not lack courage. I might spare

your life. Bring me the daughter of the Green Emperor within ten days and you shall go free. Otherwise, wherever you are and however closely you are guarded, be sure that my hooves will dash out your brains and my fangs will tear out your throat.'

Aleodor felt that he had no choice, even if he also felt that he had little chance. He mounted his restless horse and, solemnly promising to perform the service in exchange for his life, galloped off along the track ahead of him.

After a while he found himself riding beside a lake and was surprised to see, a little way in front of him, a stranded pike thrashing around in the shallows.

Aleodor suddenly realized that he was feeling hungry and thought the pike would make a good meal. But as he dismounted to scoop it on to the shore, the pike spoke:

'Only spare my life, handsome youth,' it said, 'and I promise to do you as good a service in return.'

Aleodor felt pity for the stranded creature and lifted it back into the deeper water.

The pike twisted its body against a rock, dislodging a scale from its side.

'Take this scale,' it said. 'Whenever you look at it and think of me, I shall come to your aid.' And with that, the pike plunged into the depths of the lake.

The young Emperor was travelling on, still lost in amazement at this strange encounter, when his attention was caught by a bird flapping helplessly in his path. He saw that it was a rook with a broken wing.

'If I can't have a pike to eat,' said Aleodor, springing down from his horse, 'I suppose I must make do with a rook.' At this, the rook stopped flapping and spoke.

'Only spare my life, handsome youth,' it said, 'and I promise to do you as good a service in return.'

Aleodor felt pity for the helpless creature, and gently straightened out its broken wing with a small splint made from a twig and a short length of creeper. He then lifted the bird to the safety of a dense bush. The rook flicked its tail against a branch, dislodging a feather.

'Take this feather,' it said. 'Whenever you look at it and think of me I shall come to your aid.' And he disappeared into the leafy depths of the bush.

Aleodor travelled on, quite overcome with wonder at these two encounters. Presently he heard the sound of running water and saw, just ahead of him, a small spring trickling from the rock.

'If I can't eat, at least I can slake my thirst,' he said, preparing to dismount.

'Please take care!' came a tiny voice from below his right foot. 'If you put your foot on the ground you will crush me to death.

'Only spare my life, handsome youth,' it continued, 'and I promise to do you as good a service in return.'

The young Emperor hastily slipped back into the saddle and peered down. He could just make out a little flying ant, struggling in the mud, right where his boot would have landed.

Aleodor felt pity for the helpless creature and, easing the horse to one side, leapt down and rescued the ant by sliding a leaf beneath it. Then he shook the flying ant gently on to the grass by the path.

The ant scratched one of its wings against a little thorn, tearing off a tiny corner.

'Take this fragment of wing,' it said. 'Whenever you look at it and think of me I shall come to your aid.' And it disappeared into the thick grass.

Aleodor, even more astonished, drank his fill, remounted his horse and continued along the track.

As night was falling, he found himself at the great gate in the wall surrounding the palace of the Green Emperor.

He knocked at the door and waited for someone to ask him his business there, but nobody came.

He waited there all night. He stood there all the next day; but nobody came. He stood there all the *next* day, but still nobody came. 'Time is passing,' he thought, with a heavy heart.

At dawn on the third day, however, the Green Emperor looked out from a window and thundered, 'What kind of servants do I keep that they let a stranger stand night and day at my gates without asking him what he wants?'

The servants all looked ashamed and two of them were quickly dispatched to escort the stranger into the Green Emperor's presence.

'What do you want, my son?' demanded the Green Emperor. 'Why do you wait so long at the gates of our court?'

Aleodor swallowed hard before he spoke. 'I have come, mighty Emperor, to seek your daughter.'

'Good,' said the Emperor, smiling. 'Very good. But first we must make a compact together, for such is our custom. You shall hide yourself wherever you think fit, three times. If my daughter finds you each time, your head will be struck from your body and impaled on a stake. Yonder you see that there is only one of the hundred stakes that does not yet bear a suitor's head.

'If, however, my daughter fails to find you, you shall receive her from me with my blessing. Consider carefully.'

'I have considered,' said the young Emperor; 'let us make our compact.'

And so the deeds were drawn up and signed and sealed, and

the Green Emperor summoned his daughter.

She stood looking at Aleodor for some time, and when she spoke there was no emotion in her voice.

'Hide where you will, young man,' she said, 'I shall find you. For I can see where no other human eyes can see.'

The Green Emperor struck the ground with his imperial staff, at which all the members of the court melted away, leaving Aleodor to choose his hiding place. And all the time he was thinking about the ninety-nine heads on the ninety-nine stakes.

He explored the palace, he crept about the grounds, but every possible hiding-place seemed far too obvious. Just as he was about to give up in despair, he remembered his remarkable adventures on the road.

Sitting down on the rim of one of the garden fountains, he plunged his fingers into his pocket. He brought out the fish scale, placed it in the palm of his hand and conjured up a picture of its owner in his mind's eye.

Immediately the pike raised his head from the fountain pool. 'Tell me how I can help you, handsome youth,' it said.

Aleodor explained his predicament and begged the pike to lend his assistance.

'I shall do what I can,' he heard it say, and before he knew what was happening he was borne away in a rushing of wind and a swirling of water.

When it was time for the Green Emperor's daughter to begin her search she stepped on to her balcony and looked to left and looked to right.

A puzzled expression crossed her face. 'All the other unfortunates hid themselves in the cellars or in the barn lofts or in the haystacks,' she said to herself, 'but you have done something better than that, young man.'

And she took her magic eye-glass from around her neck and

scanned the palace and grounds.

'Ah, ha!' she cried at last, 'I have found you; but I must confess you have given me much trouble to do so, for you have made yourself into a mussel lying on the sandy bottom of the sea.' And she clicked her fingers.

At once the young Emperor was transported from his hiding place in the depths of the ocean and changed back into his human shape.

'You have found me at once,' he said, and hung his head.

'Father,' she said, 'this youth is not like the others.'

'We shall see tomorrow,' said the Green Emperor.

The next day Aleodor slipped into the shrubbery and took the feather from his pocket. As soon as he began to gaze on it and think about its owner, the rook appeared on a branch above his head.

'Tell me how I can help you, handsome youth,' it said.

Aleodor explained his predicament and begged the rook to lend his assistance.

'I shall do what I can,' he heard it say, and then he found himself being swept into the air and blown about the skies.

The Green Emperor's daughter stood on her balcony with her magic eye-glass, scanning the palace grounds.

'Ah, ha!' she cried at last, 'but better and better, young man.

'So you thought to trick me by turning into a baby rook flying among the flock of rooks, did you?' And she clicked her fingers.

At once the young Emperor was transported from his hiding place in the air and changed back into his human shape.

'You have found me twice,' he said, and hung his head.

The Green Emperor's daughter turned to her father. 'Has the young man not shown remarkable skill?' she said.

'Indeed he has,' he replied, 'and I long to know where he will hide himself tomorrow - for our contract says that he must hide, and you must find him, three times.'

The next day, Aleodor slipped into a barn and delicately took the fragment of ant's wing from his pocket. As soon as he began to gaze on it and think about its owner, the flying ant appeared among the chaff on the floor.

'Tell me how I can help you, handsome youth,' it said.

Aleodor explained his predicament and begged the flying ant to lend his assistance.

'There were only three chances, and today is the third and last,' he urged.

'I shall do what I can,' Aleodor heard the ant say, and then he found himself being blown across the barn floor and along the gravel paths.

The Emperor's daughter stood on her balcony with her magic eye-glass, scanning the palace and grounds.

But she couldn't see the young Emperor. She peered far and wide, high and low, but still she couldn't see him. All day she looked, growing more and more bewildered.

Then, as the light was beginning to fade she came down into the garden where her father was waiting.

'I shall find him in a minute,' she said. 'I know he is near. Very near. But where exactly can he be?'

A gong sounded. Time had run out.

The Green Emperor smiled, pulled the contract from his pocket and solemnly tore it in two.

'Reveal yourself, young man,' he said, 'for you have won our contest, and have won my daughter.'

'Yes, reveal yourself,' said his daughter, still amazed.

'Then kindly shake your skirts,' came a small voice from somewhere near the ground.

The Green Emperor's daughter carefully shook the hem of her

skirt and saw a tiny flower seed drop on to the gravel path.

Immediately Aleodor was changed back into his human shape.

'You didn't find me the third time,' he said, and looked her straight in the eye.

There was great rejoicing in the palace that night and great feasting. The Green Emperor would have ordered a month of celebrations, but the young man was so insistent that he must depart the next day that the Emperor had to agree to his wishes.

Before the assembled court he formally presented his daughter to the youth, and escorted them to the boundary of his empire with great ceremony.

It should have been a moment of immense happiness for Aleodor, but his heart was heavy with grief at what was to come. He was a man of his word, though, and had made a solemn vow to bring the Green Emperor's daughter to the Half-man-half-lame-horse.

The moment that the young Emperor had been fearing came when they stopped to take a drink at a clear spring. The Green Emperor's daughter put her arms around him and told him how relieved she had been that he had won the contest and had won her hand in marriage.

Aleodor released himself from her embrace. 'Please find it in your heart to forgive me,' he begged. 'When I told our father that I had come to seek his daughter, I should have said that it was not for myself but for someone else.' And he hung his head and looked wretched.

'If only you had told me so when I was at home,' she said, with no anger in her voice, 'I would have known what to do. But what's past is past and perhaps, even now, all is not lost.'

They travelled on in silence after that until they came to the territory of the Half-man-half-lame-horse. As soon as he heard their horses approaching, he rushed out to claim his prize.

Brave though she was, the Green Emperor's daughter hid behind Aleodor, while the deformed creature tried to induce her to go with him to his lair. 'For you are an Emperor's daughter,' he slobbered, 'and you shall be treated like an Emperor's daughter, my dear. You shall have fresh straw to lie on every fortnight and as many roots as you care to eat. Only let me hear you say that you'll be my loving wife.'

She dropped lightly from her horse. With head held high, she

said, 'I know the man I desire to marry. If I cannot marry him I shall marry no one. And I shall certainly never marry *you*.'

'You are making me angry, my dear,' spluttered the Half-man-half-lame-horse, tottering from side to side in an agitated way. 'And it doesn't do to make me angry, you know. You might regret it.'

'I regret nothing,' said the Green Emperor's daughter, taking a long branch and drawing a wide circle in the dust around her feet.

'Obstinate and strong-willed, are you?' snarled the Half-man-half-lame-horse. 'Then I'll have to break your will. If you won't give me your hand, I'll just have to take it.'

Aleodor was just about to leap down and attack the horrible creature when a look from the Green Emperor's daughter told him to hold back.

'We'll see who's strong-willed!' slavered the monster, hurling himself clumsily towards his prize.

But as he did so, the earth opened along the circle around the Green Emperor's daughter, forming a great gap that the spitting creature could not cross, no matter how hard he tried. He raved, he fumed, he screeched, until finally, so overcome was he with fury and shame that such a gentle creature should have got the better of him, he burst with rage.

The earth closed up, and Aleodor was able to reclaim his bride-to-be.

When his anxious people saw him returning safe and sound, they cheered as they had never cheered before. They took the radiant Green Emperor's daughter to their hearts and made her feel that she had truly come home.

The young Emperor and Empress soon produced a family, and it warmed the people's hearts to hear the sounds of young voices around the palace. And you can be sure that, though the distant mountain was now quite safe, no one ever set foot on it again.

THE
PUMPKIN TREE

West Indies

THERE WAS ONCE a poor widow who had six hungry children to feed. Early every morning she used to sling a sack over her shoulder and go out looking for something to eat.

One day, she saw a very old man sitting on a log by the river.

'Good morning, mother,' said the old man.

'And good morning to you, father,' said the widow.

'If you have a little time to spare, would you be kind enough to wash my hair for me?' asked the old man.

Well, the widow didn't really have much time to spare as it took so long to collect roots and berries to feed her hungry family. But she felt sorry for the poor old man, so she said she'd be pleased to wash his hair for him.

When she had finished, he thanked her very kindly and held out a small coin. The widow hesitated. 'You don't have to pay me,' she said. 'I was pleased to be able to help you.'

'Do your children like pumpkins?' asked the old man.

'My children love pumpkins,' said the widow.

'In that case,' said the old man, 'take the coin and walk along

that path there. After a while you'll come to a tall tree covered in pumpkins. It's a magic pumpkin tree. Dig a small hole at its root and bury the coin there. Then, whenever you want any pumpkins, just call for as many as you like.'

The widow told him how grateful she was, and trotted off along the track.

There, sure enough, was the tall pumpkin tree covered in pumpkins. She got down on her knees, scrabbled away some loose earth, and buried the coin. Then she stood up to think what to do next.

'I mustn't be greedy,' she told herself. 'I'll ask for just enough pumpkins to keep the children well fed and happy.'

So, 'Six pumpkins, please,' was what she said.

To her delight, six beautifully ripe pumpkins floated down and landed gently at her feet. She gathered them into her sack and panted off back home. There she boiled them and sat down with her children to the best meal they'd ever had.

And every morning she was able to leave enough boiled pumpkin to keep the children contented until she returned from her work.

One day, to her surprise, she found a baby on the doorstep. 'The poor little mite looks hungry,' she said, 'but it will be no trouble to care for it and feed it - as long as it likes pumpkin.'

So the good-hearted soul changed her request to the magic pumpkin tree. 'Seven pumpkins, please,' was what she said now.

After a while she began to notice that all the boiled pumpkin had been eaten up and the pot licked clean when she returned from her work. And yet her children were still hungry.

'But I left you enough boiled pumpkin,' she said.

'We know,' they replied, 'but the baby eats it all.'

'The baby!' she exclaimed. 'That's nonsense; a little baby can't eat all that much boiled pumpkin.'

'We know,' they said. 'But, all the same, he does.'

The widow made a plan. The next morning, while the baby was still asleep in his cot, she sent the children to play in the fields. Then she rigged a big wicker bird trap above the pot of pumpkin. If anyone touched the pot, the trap would catch him. She was a wily old widow.

Later, when she came back to the hut with her children, she heard a howling and a bawling.

'Let me out! Let me out!' It was the baby, caught in the trap.

'I'll let you out, and turn you out,' said the widow, hauling the baby out of the trap. 'There's gratitude for you, trying to eat me out of house and home. I've a good mind to give you a smacked-bottom!'

But she never did because, to her amazement, the baby suddenly turned into a hefty young man with a very disagreeable look on his face.

All the children hid behind their mother's skirts as the brawny fellow snorted in annoyance and stormed off towards the river. There he saw the very old man.

'What's all this about a magic pumpkin tree?' demanded the bad-tempered young man.

'Ah, the magic pumpkin tree,' sighed the old man. 'I don't suppose you have time to stay and wash my hair for me, do you?' he asked.

'Whether I have the time or not, I don't intend to do it,' shouted the young man, with an even more disagreeable look on his face. 'Just tell me where the magic pumpkin tree is.'

The very old man pointed a gnarled finger at the path, and the young man tramped off without so much as a thank you.

When he reached the magic tree, he gazed up at the plump, ripe pumpkins with greedy eyes.

'Now one would probably be enough to be going on with,' he thought, 'but why leave so many on the tree, tempting other people to steal them from me? No, I think I'd better take ten.'

So he looked up into the branches of the magic pumpkin tree and yelled, 'Ten pumpkins, and be quick about it!'

And, sure enough, ten pumpkins came hurtling down on his head and crushed him to death.

THE OLD MAN AND THE JINNI

Iraq

IN THE FAR distant past, in a little village, there lived an old man and his wife. He had worked hard all his life for very little reward, but now times were hard indeed and he was often forced to beg.

To add to his misfortune, his wife, who had always had a sharp tongue, constantly shouted at him and accused him of being lazy.

'You idle wretch,' she shrieked at him one morning. 'There's not so much as a crust of bread in the place, and yet you never trouble yourself to look for more work. Oh no! You couldn't care less if we starved to death!'

All this was untrue and unfair, but the old man knew better than to argue with his wife.

'I'll see if I can find someone to hire me, dear,' he said, as he left.

'Woe betide you if you don't!' she shouted after him.

But in the village no one would employ him; the harvest was finished and, anyway, he looked so frail.

And then a thought occurred to him. 'Why don't I journey to the town?' he asked himself. 'I shall never find work here, and my wife will only scream and shout if I return without a job. But in the town I might find someone to hire me.'

And so he trudged on towards the town, through the heat of the day. Just as he was becoming very thirsty he saw a well shaded with trees a little way ahead.

He took a drink of cool water and settled down in the shade to rest his weary feet. But he hadn't been resting long before he saw a cloud of dust coming over the brow of the hill.

His heart turned to jelly. His wife was following him!

'Don't think I haven't been watching you!' she screamed, as she approached. 'I saw you slinking off to the town to have a good time, leaving me to waste away without so much as a bone to gnaw at.'

Instinctively he put up his arm to ward off the blows as she pummelled him about the shoulders with her fists.

But the ground was stony and uneven. She lost her footing and fell head over heels into the well.

'I must try to get her out,' thought the old man, in a panic. But then he reconsidered: 'Perhaps fate meant her to fall down the well and leave me free to find a new life in the city.'

And so, just in case fate should change its mind, he set off along the track again. He hadn't gone far before he heard faint cries in the air and, looking back, saw that another cloud of dust was approaching.

His heart sank. 'I thought it was too good to be true,' he said, preparing himself for the worst.

But it was not his wife. It was a jinni, and he was very angry. 'I have come to slay you,' he hissed.

The old man fell to his knees. 'Why should you wish to slay such a miserable wretch as me?' he quaked. 'In what way have I offended Your Greatness?'

'For fifty years I have slumbered peacefully in that well,' boomed the jinni. 'Until today, when you flung in that she-devil whose tongue is like a whiplash and whose voice is like the screeching of peacocks!'

'Then you should have mercy, O Great One,' said the old man.

'Consider: you have had fifty years of peace and quiet, and only one hour of my wife's scolding, but I have had fifty years of my wife's scolding and only one hour of peace and quiet. Surely I deserve your pity?'

'Your lot has indeed been hard,' said the jinni, 'but the fact remains that your wife is in my well.'

'Then why not leave her there, and travel the world with me?' asked the old man, amazed at his own boldness.

The jinni was highly amused by the idea and agreed to accompany the old man to the town. He treated him to the best meal he had ever eaten in his life, and rented a large house with an army of attentive servants. Gold is never a problem for a jinni.

For a few months they lived there happily, but one day the jinni, with a serious look on his face, took the old man aside.

'We must part now, my friend,' he said, 'for if we continue to live together, I will surely do you great harm. It is in the nature of a jinni to make mischief and destroy happiness, and I would not wish to bring further misfortune on a good friend.'

'Alas,' said the old man, 'how shall I do without money?'

'I shall bestow a parting gift on you, in return for a promise,' said the jinni, 'and by that gift you will secure fame and fortune for yourself.'

'It is my special delight to enter people's brains and drive them mad. When I leave you I intend to go to the capital and get into the brain of the daughter of the grand wazir. He is a very rich man, and desperately fond of his daughter, so he will give a generous reward to the person who can cure the possessed girl.'

'And you will teach me how to cure her?' asked the old man.

'On one condition,' said the jinni slyly: 'that you will never use this spell against me again. I swear that if you do I shall enter *your* brain in revenge, and make the end of your days an absolute torment.'

If you have any sense, you will never say anything to offend a jinni, and so the old man agreed to keep to the terms of the bargain. Hearing this, the jinni taught him the words of the magic spell and then disappeared.

It came as no surprise to the old man when he reached the capital, to hear that the grand wazir's daughter had fallen seriously ill and that the wazir's own doctors had been unable to cure her.

The old man plucked up his courage and presented himself at the wazir's house, saying that he was a skilled physician from distant parts.

The wazir received him courteously but asked him if he really felt confident that he could cure a girl who seemed to be possessed by an evil spirit.

'I am absolutely confident, your honour, but I must demand a high fee for my services.'

'Name it,' said the wazir. 'Our daughter is more precious to us than riches.'

'My price is two thousand gold coins,' said the old man.

'Two thousand gold coins!' the wazir roared. 'That is outrageous! I shall try every physician in the country before I employ you. Be off, and thank your stars for having got off so lightly for your impertinence.'

The old man bowed and went away quietly.

The poor girl's condition grew worse, day by day. More doctors came and advised every different kind of cure. She had poultices laid on her brow, she was taken to the salt springs, she was anointed with balms and salves. But still she tossed and turned, moaned and raved.

The grand wazir sent for the old man.

'Cure her,' he said. 'I shall pay your price.'

'Ah,' said the old man; 'my fee has increased, your honour. It is now one half of your possessions.'

The wazir roared even louder than before. 'Men have been whipped to within an inch of their lives for less than this! Remove yourself from my sight. There is yet a hermit from the hills. He shall cure my daughter, you rogue!'

The old man bowed and went away quietly.

The hermit was summoned, came, burned herbs and spices all about the room, and left the wretched girl ranting and wailing more feverishly than before. The grand wazir sent for the old man again.

'Cure her,' he pleaded. 'I shall pay you half I possess.'

'Your honour,' said the old man, 'my fee has increased. It is now one half of your possessions and the hand of your daughter.'

'I shall pay what you ask,' said the grand wazir in a stony voice. 'But see to it that the cure is perfect. If not, you can expect no more than a sound beating from my servants.'

The old man was shown into the room of the wazir's daughter. It pained him deeply to see how the handmaidens had bound her tightly to her bed with cords of silk to stop her injuring herself.

Once he was left alone in the room with her, he whispered the magic words. Instantly she screamed and the jinni was expelled from her mouth as a puff of black smoke which disappeared out of the window.

The old man loosened the cords and led the smiling, grateful girl, fully restored to health, to where her father waited anxiously outside.

'This good man has delivered me from my prison of torment, father,' she said. 'He must be richly rewarded.'

When the grand wazir explained what had been agreed, she said that she would be delighted to be the wife of such a man. And so all three were happy.

The old man and his new wife lived in luxury in one of the

grandest houses in the city. As they sat, cross-legged, drinking coffee on their balcony one day, the old man said to his wife, 'My life until this time had been one of perpetual misery, but now I see nothing but happiness before me.'

He had spoken too soon. The grand wazir was announced and addressed his son-in-law courteously.

'The greatest of all honours is about to be bestowed on you,' he said. 'The Khalifa has commanded me to take you to his palace, where his unfortunate daughter has just been possessed by a malicious spirit. The Khalifa, in his generosity, grants you permission to cure her.'

The old man was truly alarmed, for he guessed this was his jinni up to his wicked tricks again. If he refused to go to the palace, the Khalifa would punish him; but if he used the spell again, the jinni's punishment would be worse.

In the end, protesting that his skills were still imperfect, he allowed himself to be escorted to the palace.

'We grant you leave to cure our daughter at once,' ordered the Khalifa.

'My lord, I beg you to send for your court physicians first; my knowledge is very limited,' stammered the old man.

'What!' thundered the Khalifa. 'You cure the daughter of my grand wazir and, pleading modesty, you refuse to cure the daughter of the Khalifa himself! Such modesty tempts the executioner's axe. You *will* cure my daughter!'

The wretched old man was taken under guard to the room of the Khalifa's daughter and thrown in.

As he looked at her, he thought of the misery that he had brought upon himself, and a little tear ran down his cheek. Then suddenly his eyes lit up. His joints were weak, but his brain was still alert. 'What an idiot I'm being,' he said to himself. 'Of course, there's a way out!'

Stepping closer to the bed, he boldly pronounced the magic spell. Instantly the daughter of the Khalifa screamed and the jinni was expelled from her mouth as a puff of black smoke.

But he didn't disappear out of the window. Instead, he hovered in front of the old man. 'You old fool!' he hissed. 'Don't say I didn't warn you. I was just settling down to a very pleasant time, tormenting this girl, but you had to spoil it. Well, you've asked for it. I am going to enter *you* now, and rack your broken body and brain for the rest of your wretched life.'

'O Great One,' said the old man sadly, 'a few days ago, when I was truly happy, your threat would have terrified me, I have to confess. But now my wife has escaped from the well and has come to join me here. I fear you cannot make my wretched life any more wretched.'

The black smoke turned decidedly pale.

'Your wife?' it gasped. 'Escaped from the well? No, I'm not going to listen to her constant screeching and nagging! No, no! Anything but that!' And he swirled out of the window like a hurricane and was never seen or heard of in those parts again.

So the old man spent the rest of his days in contentment with his loving wife after all.